Little Black
Goes to
the Circus

By Walter Farley

WITH ILLUSTRATIONS BY
James Schucker

Beginner Books, a division of Random House, Inc.

This title was originally catalogued by the Library of Congress as follows: Farley, Walter. Little Black goes to the circus. With illus. by James Schucker. [New York] Beginner Books [1963] 59 p. col. illus. 24 cm. "B-33." I. Title. PZ7.F236Lk 63-13866 ISBN 0-394-80033-8 ISBN 0-394-90033-2 (lib. bdg.)

For Tim, who helped write it.

I call my pony Little Black.

He and I are good friends.

Little Black will do anything for me.

He will do tricks for me.
He will open a gate.

He will jump over things.
When he is tired of tricks,
he gets down.
Then I get on his back
and we go for rides.

One day, we went for a long ride.
We came to a man
putting up a sign.
It said BRUNO'S CIRCUS.
The circus was coming to town.

"Come on, Little Black," I said.

"Let's see the circus.

Let's see it come to town."

Little Black ran very fast.
Soon we came to the circus tents.
We saw circus wagons.
Then we saw circus animals
and circus people.

We saw Mr. Bruno.

Mr. Bruno said to his men,

"Come on!

Get the animals out!"

Then Mr. Bruno worked
with the animals.
He made them do tricks.
He made a monkey
ride a little bike.

Next, he worked
with an elephant.
He made that big elephant
get up on a little box.

Then he worked with a pony.
Mr. Bruno made him
walk on two feet.
He made that pony
walk across the ring.

14

All at once, Little Black jumped up.

He got up on his two feet,

just like the circus pony!

Mr. Bruno looked up in surprise.

"What is this?" he asked

"What is going on here?"

Then Little Black fell down!

He fell down hard.

All the circus people laughed.

"Take that pony away,"
said Mr. Bruno.
"He is no good!
He is no circus pony.
Get him out of here!"

I took Little Black away.

I had to pull him.

His head was down.

His tail was down.

"Don't be sad, Little Black,"
I said. "You are a good pony.
Mr. Bruno does not know a
good pony when he sees one."

I wanted to make my pony happy.

"Little Black," I said,

"let's have our own circus."

"I know a new trick
you can do.
I bet you can walk
across this plank.
Come on. Try it."

"Come on. Come on.
Don't stop!
Keep going, Little Black!
You will do it!"

"You did it!
You are a good pony.
You are just as good
as any circus pony."

Then Little Black pulled away.

He ran!

"Little Black," I called,

"where are you going?

Come back! Come back!"

I ran after him.

I ran as fast as I could.

But Little Black ran faster.

He was going back to the circus!

"Stop!" I yelled.

But Little Black ran on.

He ran right into the big tent.

I ran into the big tent, too.

All the circus people

were looking at something.

What had happened to my pony?

There he was!

He was on a plank.

There was Mr. Bruno, too.

"Well," said Mr. Bruno,

"that pony is good."

"Now let's see
just how good you are.
Get up there.
Try your trick
on a high plank."

"Oh, no! Don't!

Please, Mr. Bruno!" I yelled.

"Little Black will fall."

"He can't fall far!
This belt will hold him.
Come on, Little Black,"
said Mr. Bruno.
"Come on! Hurry up!
Nothing will happen!"

But then . . .
something did happen.
Little Black fell!

But he did not fall far.
The belt held him up.

"Let him down!" I yelled.
But they did not do it.
They pulled him back up.

Then everything was all right.
Little Black walked
right across the plank.
I was glad it was all over.

But it was not all over.

Mr. Bruno took off the belt.

"Now," said Mr. Bruno,

"let's see you walk

back across that plank."

Little Black started.

Then he stopped.

"Don't stop!" I yelled.

"You will fall!

Keep going.

Don't look down!

Please do as I say."

Little Black did as I said.

He got there!

He was so happy

he got up on his two back feet.

"You did it, Little Black!"

I yelled.

"You did the big circus trick!"

Little Black came down.

But I could not get near him.

He had a lot of friends now.

Now they did not laugh at him.

"Little Black," said Mr. Bruno,
"I will make you the star
of my circus!"

I went out of the tent.

I sat down to think.

My pony wanted to stay
with the circus.

He wanted to be a circus star.

I did not want to let him go.

But I wanted him to be happy.

I did not know what to do.

Then I heard something.

I looked up.

It was Little Black!

He came running
out of the tent.
He was running away
from the circus.
He was running to me!

He stopped.

He got down.

He wanted me to get on his back.

He did not want to stay
with the circus.

He wanted to go home with me.

59

We ran. We jumped.
We did tricks
all the way home.
It was hard to tell
who was happier,
Little Black or I.